STEP INTO READING® will help your child get there. The program offers five steps to reading success. Each step includes fun stories and colorful art or photographs. In addition to original fiction and books with favorite characters, there are Step into Reading Non-Fiction Readers, Phonics Readers and Boxed Sets, Sticker Readers, and Comic Readers—a complete literacy program with something to interest every child.

Learning to Read, Step by Step!

Ready to Read **Preschool–Kindergarten**
• big type and easy words • rhyme and rhythm • picture clues
For children who know the alphabet and are eager to begin reading.

Reading with Help **Preschool–Grade 1**
• basic vocabulary • short sentences • simple stories
For children who recognize familiar words and sound out new words with help.

Reading on Your Own **Grades 1–3**
• engaging characters • easy-to-follow plots • popular topics
For children who are ready to read on their own.

Reading Paragraphs **Grades 2–3**
• challenging vocabulary • short paragraphs • exciting stories
For newly independent readers who read simple sentences with confidence.

Ready for Chapters **Grades 2–4**
• chapters • longer paragraphs • full-color art
For children who want to take the plunge into chapter books but still like colorful pictures.

STEP INTO READING® is designed to give every child a successful reading experience. The grade levels are only guides; children will progress through the steps at their own speed, developing confidence in their reading. The F&P Text Level on the back cover serves as another tool to help you choose the right book for your child.

Remember, a lifetime love of reading starts with a single step!

For Morty

Visit us on the Web!
StepIntoReading.com
rhcbooks.com

Educators and librarians, for a variety of teaching tools, visit us at RHTeachersLibrarians.com

Library of Congress Cataloging-in-Publication Data is available upon request.
ISBN 978-0-593-43464-2 (trade) — ISBN 978-0-593-43465-9 (lib. bdg.) —
ISBN 978-0-593-43466-6 (ebook)

Printed in the United States of America
10 9 8 7 6 5 4 3 2 1

This book has been officially leveled by using the F&P Text Level Gradient™ Leveling System.

STEP INTO READING®

GRUMPY MONKEY

The Egg-Sitter

by Suzanne Lang
illustrated by Max Lang

Random House New York

It was a nice day.
It was not too hot
or too cold.

Jim Panzee was happy.
There were so many
fun things to do
on a day like this.

Jim ran into
Oxpecker and
Water Buffalo.
Oxpecker had an egg.

"Can you watch my egg
for me, Jim?"
Oxpecker asked.
"All you have to do
is sit on it."

Sitting on an egg
did not sound fun
to Jim.
He did not want to
be an egg-sitter.

But before he could
say something,
they left.
"Thank you, Jim!"
called Oxpecker.

Now Jim was stuck
with the egg.
He sat on it.
And sat.
And sat.

And sat.

Oxpecker was taking

a long time.

Jim was very bored.

Then his friends
Norman and Leslie
came by.
"What are you doing?"
asked Norman.

“Egg-sitting,” said Jim.
“Sounds boring,”
said Norman.
“It is,” said Jim.
“I cannot enjoy this
nice day.”

“If we take turns sitting
on the egg,”
said Norman,
“you will get
to have
some fun.”

First Norman sat on the egg.

Jim and Leslie played tag.

Then Leslie sat on the egg.

Jim and Norman splashed.

Jim was happy.
He got to have fun
after all.

It was time for lunch.
Leslie picked leaves.
Jim and Norman
ate bananas.

“Wait!” said Jim.
“No one is sitting on
the egg!”

The friends looked

for the egg.

They could not find it.

Oxpecker and
Water Buffalo
came back.
Oxpecker was upset.
"You lost my egg!"
she cried.

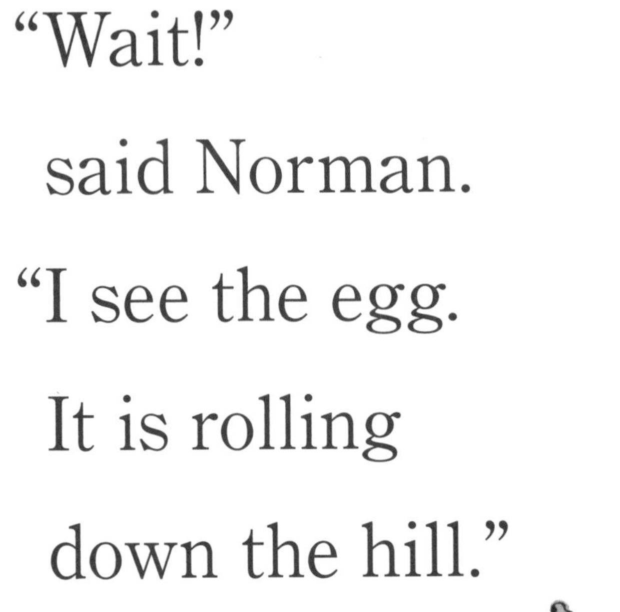

"Wait!"
said Norman.
"I see the egg.
It is rolling
down the hill."

Jim ran after it.

The egg rolled
into Snake's nest.
No one knew
which egg
was Oxpecker's.

Snake was hungry.
She asked Jim to watch
the eggs.
"You do not sit on
snake eggs.
You hug them," Snake said.

Jim hugged the eggs.

One of the eggs cracked.

It was a baby bird!

“My baby!” said Oxpecker.

“Mama,” said the baby bird to Oxpecker.

Then the other eggs cracked.
All the baby snakes looked at Jim.
"Mama!" they all said.

"This is the last time I egg-sit!" said Jim.